THE USBORNE BOOK OF
JOKES

written and compiled by
Philip Hawthorn
Designed by Russell Punter
Illustrated by Kim Blundell

What's got two humps and is found on the moon?

A lost camel.

Turn over the page to find out!

WHAT'S THIS?

First published in 1991 by Usborne Publishing Ltd, Usborne House, 83-85 Saffron Hill, London EC1N 8RT, England. Copyright © 1991 Usborne Publishing Ltd. The name Usborne and the device ✲ are Trade Marks of Usborne Publishing Ltd. All rights reserved. No part of this publication may be reproduced, stored in a retrieval system or transmitted in any form or by any means, electronic, mechanical, photocopying, recording or otherwise, without the prior permission of the publisher. Printed in Belgium.

Did you hear about the stupid ghost? He bumped into a door.

Why do witches ride on broomsticks? Because vacuum cleaners haven't got long enough cords.

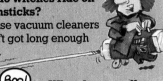
Boo!

What do you call a ghostly feline? Scaredy-cat.

What do you get if you cross a Boy Scout with a monster? Something that scares old ladies across the road.

What has webbed feet and fangs? Count Quackula.

What was the skeleton gangster called? Al Ca-bone.

Why do pyramids have horns instead of doorbells? So you can toot-and-come-in.

Is mummy in?

How do you get into a locked coffin? Using a skeleton key.

DOCTOR DOCTOR

I think I'm dead. It must be the coffin.

Lazy bones.

I like a nice skele-tan.

There once was a woman from Ryde,
Who ate ninety apples and died.
The apples fermented
Inside the lamented,
And made cider inside 'er inside.

Where do American Indian ghosts live? In a creepy teepee.

Heard the joke about the snow-ghost? You'll be scared stiff.

Haunted Housemusic

What dance do ghosts do best? Boo-gie.

What do you get if you cross a monster with a canary? A big yellow thing that goes "TWEET!!"

Tweet!

This is my family photograph.

I can't tell witch is witch.

NEWSFLASH
All the ghosts in England are on strike. Here's a report from our spooksman.

What's strong and miserable? The Incredible Sulk

What's the first thing a monster eats after it's had a tooth out? The dentist.

A banana sneezing.

THE HAUNTED HOUSE by HUGO FIRST

INVESTIGATING GHOSTS by DENISE R. KNOCKING

DEADLY JOKES by Di Laffin

Terrible Nightmare BY GLADYS OVER

Book Worm

When will I die? BY Sue Nora Later

FAMOUS FRIGHTS by TERRY FIED

That's Wick-ed!

What's the smelliest game?
Ping pong.

Why are babies good at soccer?
Because they are expert dribblers.

What's got feathers, ticks and is hit regularly?
A shuttle-clock.

What do you call a broken go-kart?
A stop-kart.

What's an electric eel's favourite game?
Ice shock-ey.

What's blue and furry, and does 80mph?
A cold gerbil on skis.

What's the difference between a bad wrestler and a bad electrician?
One loses fights, the other fuses lights.

When are racing cars like cats?
When they are lapping.

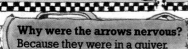

What a purr-fect joke.

Why were the arrows nervous?
Because they were in a quiver.

What do you get if you cross a chess piece with Chinese food?
A pawn cracker.

If you have an umpire in tennis and a referee in football, what do you get in bowls?

Goldfish.

Why are baseball fields so valuable?
Because they have a diamond in the middle.

What ring is square?
A boxing ring.

DOCTOR DOCTOR

I'm a wrestler and I feel awful.
Get a grip on yourself.

I think I'm a tennis racket.
You're too highly strung.

I keep thinking I'm a pack of cards.
Sit down and I'll deal with you later.

I keep thinking I'm a billiard ball.
Get to end of the cue.

My nose keeps running.
Well lock it up then.

NEWSFLASH

Rex, the champion dog, is missing. Police say they have no lead on him.

KNOCK! KNOCK! WHO'S THERE?

Judo.
Judo who?
Judo I gotta cold.

JO JITSU Martial Arts Instructor

Did you hear about the man who went fly fishing?
He caught a 3lb bluebottle.

What's a jockey's favourite country?
Horse-tralia

Why don't giants like polo?
Because they prefer po-high.

Why does a golfer carry two pairs of trousers?
In case he gets a hole in one.

Why did two elephants not enter the swimming race?
They'd only one pair of trunks.

Why was the athlete in trouble?
Because she was for the high jump.

A worms eye view of an early bird.

WORLD'S WORST SHOT by Mrs De-Target

THE RACE by Willie Wynn and Betty Does

I've got an enormous pack of cards.

Big deal.

Mice Skating

I keep racing pigeons

Do you ever win?

How was the naughty train punished?
It had to write railway lines.

Why did the toad visit the mushroom?
Because it was a toad-school.

What do you call a vampire adding numbers?
Counter Dracula.

How do you know if a hippo is sitting next to you at school?
He has an 'H' on his pencil case.

What's a butterfly's favourite lesson?
Moth-ematics.

What disease do art teachers get?
Pencilitis.

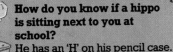

REGISTER

NAME	
Eileen	A girl with one long leg and one short leg
Oscar	A boy who is a world famous actor
Wanda	A girl who sleep walks
Claude	A boy who keeps a wild tiger
Berna-dette	A girl who throws gas bills on the fire
Beatrix	A girl who balances 3 pints of beer on her head
Cliff	A boy with a face like a rock
Ingrid	A girl with her foot in a drain
Bob	A boy who can't swim

Which English king was good at fractions?
Henry 1/8th.

What do donkeys enjoy best at school?
Ass-embly.

What sum is done underwater?
An octoplus.

What's the definition of impeccable?
Something that can't be eaten by chickens.

What's the definition of a volcano?
A mountain with hiccups.

How do mushrooms count?
On their fungus.

Why didn't you write your essay on a whale?

Do you like Kipling?

How would you spell "Rhododendron"?

What is 6x7?

What's your guinea pig's name?

Because my pen wouldn't work underwater.

I don't know I've never Kippled.

I wouldn't, I'd say "bush".

If you don't know now, you never will.

I don't know, he won't tell me.

A spider doing a pole vault.

TOP OF THE ART CLASS by Andrew Best

PLAYING MUSIC BACKWARDS by Roland Rock

BADINGLISH TEECHING by Miss Spelt

FAMOUS PEOPLE IN HISTORY by Hugh Dydd-Watt

THE CLOAKROOM THIEF by Mike Oatsgone

THE END OF SCHOOL by Wendy Belgoze

TELLING OFF BULLIES by Howard U. Lykett

HOW I CUT MY KNEE by Phil Over

GREAT EGGSPECTATIONS by Charles Chickens

My teacher loves me — she keeps putting kisses by my sums.

Why did the boy fall apart on the last day of school?

Because he'd just broken up.

What do you get if you cross a school bell with an alarm clock?

Something that wakes you up when it's time to go home.

I wish I lived 400 years ago – there wasn't so much history then.

Where was the Queen of England crowned?
On the head.

Where was Magna Carta signed?
At the bottom.

Where are the Andies?
On the end of the armies.

Where were oranges first found?
In a tree.

Name two members of the deer family.
Granny Deer & Uncle Deer.

Teacher's Pet

Name two animals that live in India.
A tiger and his sister.

Has anyone ever seen the Abominable Snowman?
Not Yettie.

Where do you find edible beetles?
Depends where you left them.

Name another flower in the Chrysanthemum family.
Chrysanthe-dad.

Lunch-pack of Notre Dame

Acting Class
I must not forget my lines
I must not forget my lines
I must not... er...

What's a slide rule?

How long can someone live without a brain?

Why did your parents call you "Exit"?

How many times have I told you to stop using your calculator?

What are you doing?

Something you use to measure ski slopes.

How old are you?

They wanted to see my name in lights.

348,789.98

Pulling a funny face.

Why was the astronomer told off?
She was always staring into space.

What term do aliens like best?
Sat-term.

SPACE keep going

Especially when they're at moon-iversity.

A. At their floppy desks.

WHAT'S THIS?

What's the most popular food in heaven?
Angel cakes.

What's hairy and sneezes?
A coconut with a cold.

What's a bee's favourite sweet?
Bumble gum.

Where do sheep eat in the summer?
At a baa-beque.

Why was the peppermint in the Olympics?
Because it was a mint-ernational.

How do shellfish take pictures?
With a clam-era.

KNOCK! KNOCK! WHO'S THERE?

Olive.
Olive who?
Olive here, let me in.

Soup.
Soup who?
Superman.

A potato.
A potato who?
A potato clock I was this morning.

Toffee.
Toffee who?
Toffee tums in a tup.

A sick note

A Fez-ant

WAITER! WAITER!

How long will my sausages be?
About five inches sir.

Why have you got food all over your jacket?
You said to lay on a feast, so I did.

Is there tomato soup on the menu?
There was, but I wiped it off.

This pie doesn't taste right.
That's why it's left.

What's red and white and goes up and down?
A tomato sandwich on a pogo stick.

What looks like half a lemon?
The other half.

What's yellow, has big teeth and lives in the refrigerator?
Butter, I lied about the teeth.

What's the definition of a redcurrant?
An embarrassed blackcurrant.

Why are bananas good gymnasts?
Because they're often in splits.

I always drink cocoa in my pyjamas.

Don't they get a bit soggy?

CHIPS FROM EXOTIC COUNTRIES by Sultan Vinegar

THE EVERLASTING ICE CREAM by Trudy Light

EGG RECIPES by Sue Flay

DOCTOR DOCTOR

I think I'm a dumpling.
You are in a stew.

I feel like a burger.
Me too. Here's some money, go and get them.

I keep thinking I'm a spoon.
Just sit there and don't stir.

I feel like an apple.
Cor!

I keep thinking I can smell pepper.
That must get up your nose.

One day I think I'm an onion, the next a tomato.
You're in a bit of a pickle, then.

What's the favourite food of . . .

A hedgehog?
A spine-apple.

I thought it was a prickled onion.

A deer?
Doe-nuts.

A drummer?
Beat-root.

A hairdresser?
Par-snips.

A bricklayer?
Wall-nuts.

A hot cat?
Mice cream.

A tea-spoon?
Lob-stir.

A washing machine?
Spin-ach.

What's red, hot and travels at 150 mph?
A turbo radish.

How do lobsters get to work?
In a taxi crab.

What's black and white and has eight wheels?
A penguin on roller skates.

Where are Chinese car horns made?
Hong King.

Why did the baby put wheels on its cradle?
Because it wanted to rock and roll.

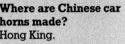

What happens to broken down frogs?
They get toad away.

How do fleas travel?
They itch-hike.

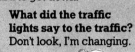

What does Corporal Goldfish drive?
A tank.

What's the difference between a big hill and a big pill?
One's hard to get up, the other's hard to get down.

What did the traffic lights say to the traffic?
Don't look, I'm changing.

How did the bride get to her wedding?
On her train.

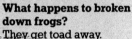

What do you call a stupid boat?
An idi-yacht.

NEWSFLASH

A ship carrying a cargo of yo-yos has hit an iceberg. It sank 46 times.

A truck carrying glue has overturned. Police say they are completely stuck.

A van loaded with strawberries has collided with another carrying sugar. There is now a huge jam.

Today some thieves hijacked a truck carrying wigs. Police are combing the area.

LONG WALK HOME by Mr. Lars Buss
OUR CAR'S BROKEN by Sarah McCannick
BREAKDOWN TRUCKS by Tony Carslately
CRASH LANDING by Claire de Runway
MY LIFE IN SUBMARINES by Perry Scope
STOLEN VEHICLES by Nick McCarr

DOCTOR DOCTOR

I've been terribly run down.
Did you get the car's number?

I feel like the back of a car.
You're exhausted.

What do you get if you cross . . .

A supersonic jet with a roll of sticky tape?
Something that breaks the sound barrier then mends it again.

A police car's light with a fried egg?
A flash in the pan.

A lake with a leaky boat?
About half way.

What did the sardine say when it saw a submarine?
Look, canned people.

What would you get if Batman and Robin were run over by a steamroller?
Flatman and Ribbon.

How do you know that planes are scared of the dark?
Because they have to leave the landing lights on.

A fried egg on a hammock.

Why did you get thrown out of the Navy?
I threw a banana skin out of the window.

They threw you out for that?
Well, I was in a submarine at the time.

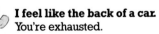

O· What's big, blue and on a diet?

What did the ballerina say in the restaurant?
A table for tu-tu.

What's short, scared of wolves and shouts "Twit-face!"
Little Rude Riding Hood.

What's the world's most musical country?
Tune-isia.

Have you heard about the chocolate factory?
When the sun came out, it melted.

Why did the broom get up in the night?
It couldn't get to sweep.

What do you get if you cross a clock with a thief?
A tick tock-et.

What do you get if you cross . . .

A computer and a banana skin?
A slipped disk.

Some grapes with a baker?
A bunch of flour.

A fridge with an angry monster?
A nasty cold.

If a red house is made of red bricks, what's a green house made of?
Glass.

Which is correct: 9+5 *is* 13, or 9+5 *are* 13?
Neither, it's 14.

That figures.

How do you catch Egyptian flu?
From mummy.

What colour was the retired trumpeter?
Blue.

What's green and goes at 150 mph?
A moss-tang.

Why did the car's wheels explode?
Because they were tyre-d out.

What's the best road on which to eat spaghetti?
One with a fork in it.

Why put your record in the refrigerator?
Because I like to play it cool.

What do you get if you leave your toothpaste in the freezer?
An ice tube.

Call me a taxi! OK – you're a taxi.

DOCTOR DOCTOR

I keep thinking I'm a spider.
Well come down off the ceiling, and let me examine you.

People keep ignoring me.
Next!

I've got invisible sickness.
I'm afraid I can't see you.

I keep getting lost.
You're telling me, this is a Chinese restaurant.

I'm a burglar and I'm sick.
Well you'd better take some medicine.

I've just swallowed a roll of film.
I'm sure nothing serious will develop.

Doctor, I've lost my memory. When did this happen?

When did what happen?

A pea on a skateboard.

THINGS TO EAT WITH *SOUP* by Roland Butter

DINNER'S READY by Carmen Geddit

LOSING WEIGHT by Wilma Clothes-Fitt

ELECTRICIANS WEEKLY ⚡ A LOOK AT CURRENT AFFAIRS

How re-volting.

What do you do if you find a crocodile in your bed?
Sleep somewhere else.

What was the baby hippo called?
Nappy-potty-mus.

What do you call horses that live next door?
Neigh-bours.

What wobbles and rings?
A jelly-phone.

What did the mouse say to its noisy children?
Squeak when you're squoken to.

What do you get if you cross a stereo with a bluebottle?
Hi-fli.

How did you stop your son from biting his nails?
I made him wear shoes.

Do you know what makes ma mad?
The letter "d".

Why did Lucy like the letter "k"?
Because it made her 'Lucky'.

I saw the sun rise today.
So what? Yesterday I saw the kitchen sink.

Do you like the carpet?
No, I wanted a van – and don't call me "pet".

DOCTOR DOCTOR

I think I'm a waste bin.
Don't talk rubbish.

I can't get to sleep.
Lie on the edge of your bed, you'll soon drop off.

KNOCK! KNOCK! WHO'S THERE?

Dishwasher.
Dishwasher who?
Dishwasher way I shpoke when losht my falshe teeff.

Ammonia.
Ammonia who?
Ammonia a little boy – I can't reach the bell.

Iona Littlemouse
Pet Street
Hamsterdam
West Gerbilly
N. Americat

Dad! There's an invisible woman at the door.
Tell her I can't see her.

Mum! There's a man with an egg at the door.
Tell him to beat it.

Mum! I've swallowed a light bulb – what shall I do?
Use a candle instead.

One of these standing on the edge of a lake.

FITTING CARPETS by Walter Wall

Baby Sitting by JUSTIN CASEY HOWLS

The NAUGHTY BOY —by— Enid Spanking

HUSH-A-BYE-BABY by Wendy Bough-breaks

SHARING A BED-ROOM by Constance Noring

AFTER THE HURRICANE —by— Rufus Quick

Where do ghosts play golf?

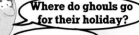

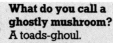

What do skeleton's put in their cakes?
Skull-tanas.

What do you call a ghost with a hose?
A fire frighter.

What's big, hairy, and goes at twice the speed of sound?
King Kongcorde.

What do you call a ghostly mushroom?
A toads-ghoul.

What do you get if you cross a barber and a ghost?
A scare-dresser.

What did the pretty ghoul enter?
A boo-ty contest.

She didn't stand a ghost of a chance.

Where do ghouls go for their holiday?
The Dead Sea.

There are always a lot of ghost-guards.

Sea-ghoul

Why are ghosts terrible liars?
You can always see through them.

NEWSFLASH

The police have appointed their first ghost. It will be called Chief In-spectre.

Today was the Monster Beauty Contest. As usual there were no winners.

What position did the ghost play at football?
Ghoulkeeper.

I keep seeing into the future.

Really, when did this start?

Next Thursday.

What's a ghost's favourite food?
Spook-hetti.

What's a ghost's favourite story?
Ghouldilocks.

What's a ghost's favourite play?
A phantomime.

What's a ghost's favourite breakfast?
Dreaded wheat.

What's a ghost's favourite sweet?
Boo-ble gum.

What are a ghost's favourite trees?
Ceme-trees.

What's a ghost's favourite game?
Hide and shriek.

I thought it was haunt the thimble.

What do ghosts say after a night's haunting?
I'm dead on my feet.

WAITER! WAITER!

What's this gravestone doing in my salad?
It's a tomb-ato.

There's a ghost in my soup.
All right sir, don't make spectre-cle of yourself.

There are some ghosts in my stew.
That's because it's ghoul-ash, sir.

His little brother.

HE RAN IN SCREAMING
by Jess C. Naspook

A HORRID DEATH
by Barry De Lyve

I SAW A SPOOK
by Claire Razz-Day

Ghost train-er

Swimming Ghoul

How does a ghoul start a letter?
Tomb it may concern.

It's delivered by the ghost-man.

22

Where do spies do their shopping?

What's black, wet and hairy?
An oil wig.

Why couldn't the man go to a Stone Age Furs exhibition?
Because it was early clothing.

Who is the patron saint of playgrounds?
St Francis of a see-saw.

What's the world's most shocking city?
Electri-city.

Where do lions buy old clothes?
Jungle sales.

What's stripy, shakes and is found at the North Pole?
A polar zebra.

DOCTOR DOCTOR

I've cut myself, and all you do is tell me jokes.
I want you to be in stitches.

I keep getting smaller.
You'll have to be little patient.

I snore so loudly that I wake myself up.
Well sleep in another room.

I've just eaten a pen.
Here's some pencillen.

My nose is running and my feet smell.
Looks like you're built upside down.

Where do sick alsatians go?
To the dog-tor.

Where do they send sick horses?
To horspital.

Where do kangeroos get their glasses?
At a Hoptitian.

KNOCK! KNOCK! WHO'S THERE?

Europe.
Europe who?
Europe early this morning.

Asia.
Asia who?
Bless you!

Jamaica.
Jamaica who?
Jamaica lot of money telling jokes?

DO NOT READ THIS NOTICE

Oi!

There was a young man from Australia,
Who painted his foot like a dahlia.
A penny a look
Was all by the book,
But sixpence a smell was a failure.

NEWSFLASH

A giant and a dwarf have just escaped from prison. Police are looking high and low for them.

At the local shops, some thieves went on the rampage. The police say that the thieves...

Stole some plant food – but they'll root them out.

Stole a mirror – and they're looking into it.

Stole a mattress – and they'll look in the spring.

Stole some soap and a sponge – then made a clean getaway.

Half of one of these.

HEALTH FOODS — CLOSED DUE TO SICKNESS

TRAVEL AGENTS — GONE ON HOLIDAY

PHOTOGRAPHERS — Back in a flash

MUSIC SHOP — BACK IN A MINUET

SHIPBUILDERS — Gone to Launch

CLOCK REPAIRS — BACK IN A TICK

Who is Santa Claus' wife?

TOYS

Custard SPY

What do you call a gun with three barrels?
A trifle.

What athlete is made of wool?
A long jumper.

Why do boomerangs never go out of fashion?
Because they're always making a comeback.

Who wears a crown and climbs ladders?
A window queen-er.

How can you cut the sea?
With a see-saw.

What's the laziest thing in a doctor's bag?
The sleeping pills.

KNOCK! KNOCK! WHO'S THERE?

Henrietta.
Henrietta who?
Henry ate a boiled egg.

Tish.
Tish who?
Got a cold?

Francis.
Francis who?
Francis full of French people.

Safari.
Safari who?
Safari so goodie.

Why didn't the clown work in the winter?
Because he only did summer-saults.

When is a clown's face like a story?
When it's made up.

How does a clown dress on a cold day?
Quickly.

What's the quickest way to the station?
Run fast.

Last night I dreamt I was talking to world's cleverest person.
Oh yes, what did I say?

This painting is over 100 years old.
Did you do it?

This morning I had to get up and answer the telephone in my pyjamas.
Funny place to have a telephone.

Your parents have got three children, haven't they?
No, only me – and two spares.

Napoleon Boneypart

THE POLICEMAN'S TEST by Courtney Crooks

What instrument is like a gun?
A bang-jo.

What's an opera star's favourite place?
Singer-pore.

Which composer ran round castles?
Moat-zart.

It was too flat.

Why wasn't the tyre allowed in the choir?

A snake doing a somersault.

What's the difference between a postbox, a canary and a fishing rod?
I don't know.

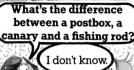

You can post a letter in a postbox but not a canary.
But what about the fishing rod?

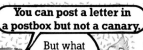

Thought that would catch you.

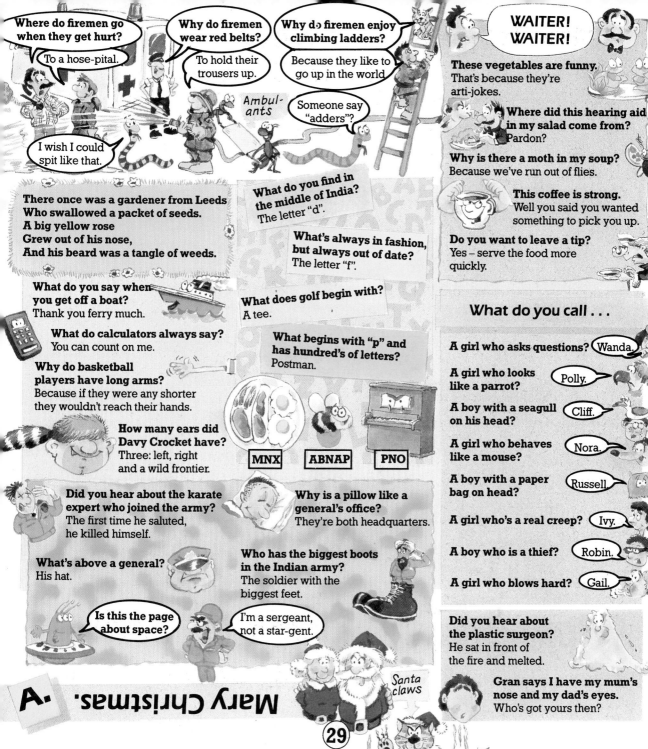

How can you create your own jokes?

On these two pages are some ideas for ways to make up your own jokes.

Jokes using a word which has two meanings

There are some words which mean two completely different things. Below is a flow chart which will help you use them to make up a joke.

| Find a word with two meanings. | A date. |

| Write down the two things that the word means in similar phrases. | A palm tree has dates. (Fruit) A calender has dates. (Days) |

| Ask why the two things are like each other to make your joke. | Why is a palm tree like a calender? Because they both have lots of dates. |

Jokes using words which sound the same, but are spelled differently.

There are also words which sound exactly the same, but which are spelled differently.

| Write down the two words. | Word 1: red Word 2: read |

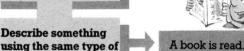

| Describe something using word 1, such as: A . . . . has a (word 1). A . . . . is (word 1). | A fire engine is red. |

| Describe something using the same type of question, and word 2. | A book is read. |

| Ask a question which includes the two things. | Why is a fire engine like a book? Because they are both read (red). |

This kind of joke works well when you say it, because the other person won't be able to see the two words are spelled differently.

Here are two lists of words which you can use to make up jokes like the ones above.

Words which have two meanings

Pen	Beam	Bank	Bill
Spring	Top	Swallow	Glasses
Stable	Post	Palm	Ball
Nail	Duck	Club	Fire
Pack	Plug	Bar	Match
Sink	Pipe	Saw	Rock
Right	Ring	Pipe	Tape
Scales	Stamp	Tip	Recorder

Words which sound the same but are spelled differently.

Queue – Cue	Bear – Bare	Fair – Fare
Right – Write	Fir – Fur	Hair – Hare
Weigh – Way	Rain – Reign	Tire – Tyre
Sail – Sale	Tale – Tail	Stair – Stare
Sun – Son	Tax – Tacks	Plain – Plane
Pair – Pear	Sore – Saw	Tow – Toe
Whole – Hole	Great – Grate	Shake – Sheik

Jokes using words which sound similar

Some jokes are funny because all or part of a word is replaced by another word which sounds like it. This is called a pun. For example: Where do rowing boats go when they are ill? To an oars-pital. Below is a flow chart which shows you how to make up pun jokes.

Write down a word which may have other words which sound similar to it. This is the Jokeword.	Quack
Write one or two new words which rhyme with it, or sound very similar.	Track Crack
Can you think of a way in which one of the new words is normally used? **No** Try again with two new words. **Yes**	Railway Tracks
Write the Jokeword in place of word 2. This will be the idea for the answer to the joke.	Railway quacks
Think up a question which uses the areas from which the two words come.	i.e. Ducks and trains **What do duck trains run on?** Railway quacks.

But you haven't said anything about space jokes.

Jokes using an 'odd' idea

You can make a joke by imagining an everyday object in an odd situation. The flow chart below tells you how.

Write down a well known object.	A plane **What it's like** Has wheels **What it does** Flies
Write two things which describe it:	
Write down an odd activity that your object could never do.	Go on a trampoline.
Describe one thing about this activity.	Bouncing up and down.
Write a joke using the three descriptions. The answer will be your original object doing the odd activity.	**What has wheels, flies and bounces up and down?** A plane on a trampoline.

Next page.

 Read these two pages.

What did the astronomer use to get out of prison?
A tel-escape.

Why was the mouse nibbling the planet?
Because it was in gnaw-bit.

What's a planet's favourite drink?
Gravi-tea.

What floats in space and looks like a donkey?
An ass-teroid.

Why are false teeth like stars?
Because they come out at night.

Where do space bees go when they get married?
On honey-moon.

SPACE INVADERS
by A. Leanne Zahir

A BUMPY TOUCH-DOWN by Paul Anding

SPACE WEAPONS BY Ray Gunne

Eggs-tra terrestrial

What's the matter with you?

I've got smelly feet.

Why is the sky high?
So birds don't bump their heads.

What bird is found in space?
A star-ling.

What do cows say at night?
Mooooon.

What do astronauts carry their sandwiches in?
A launch box.

What do you call a koala from outer space?
An austr-alien.

Where do astronauts park their spaceships?
On a parking meteor.

Why do astronauts like American football?
Because they're good at touch-downs.

What's an alien's favourite sweet?
Martian-mallows.

What fish do you find in space?
Star-fish.

How do you get a baby astronaut to sleep?
Rocket.

What's a crab's favourite planet?
Niptune.

What do space teachers always carry?
Their regi-star.

What's sweet, yellow and orbits the sun?
Mars-ipan.

What sea is in space?

The galax-sea.

What do astronauts use to play badminton with?
Space shuttle-cock.

What did the hungry astronomer say?
I'm star-ving.

Which planet is never hungry?
A full moon.

What is the most polluted planet?
Pollut-o.

What do you call a flying saucer in hot fat?
An unidentified frying object.

Why is the planet Saturn like a telephonist?
They're both surrounded by rings.

What do astronaut archers aim at?
The star-get.

What did one shooting star say to another?
Pleased to meteor.

WELCOME DAMIEN THE ALIEN!

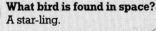

Heard any good jokes lately?

The animal jokes start here . . .

What's black and white and glows?

An electric zebra.

What animal tunnels through ice and lives in an igloo?

An eski-mole.

What's white and jumps every few seconds?

A polar bear with hiccups.

And jokes about insects, birds, reptiles, fish...

How do rich fleas travel about on their dog?
They have a chau-fur.

What did the hen say when she was pregnant?
"I'm eggs-pecting."

What's the definition of "Out Of Bounds"?
An exhausted rabbit.

What do you call the queen of the midges?
Your midge-esty.

WHAT'S THIS?

WAY OUT →

What do you call a large, angry sea-bird?
An alba-cross.

If a swan sings a swan song, what does a cygnet sing?
A signature tune.

What should you never do with a 5 ton canary?
Argue.

What lives at the South Pole and smiles?
A pen-grin.

What do you call a failed pelican?
A pelican't.

What's the definition of illegal?
A sick bird.

What bird lives in a refrigerator?
A coldfinch.

Where do storks keep their tins of baked beans?
In a stork-cupboard.

What's yellow, has twenty-two legs and goes crunch?
A canary soccer team eating crisps.

Why should you never tell a secret to a peacock?
Because they're always spreading tails.

Which are the most religious birds?
Birds of prey.

What's white and noisy?
A swan playing the bagpipes.

Where do you go to see seagull paintings?
To an art-gullery.

What's black, flies and does somersaults?
An acro-bat.

Bat-tle

Look, a wing-stand!

LARGE SEA BIRDS — by Albert Ross

What will the cockatoo be on her next birthday?
Cockathree.

What's big, white and Australian, and sits in a tree?
A cooker-burra.

What goes "Hmmm-choo?
A humming-bird with a cold.

What's black, white and red all over?
An embarrassed penguin.

What's a bee's favourite bird?
A buzz-ard.

Why did the dinosaur cross the road?
Because chickens didn't exist then.

Why do ostriches have long legs?
So you can tell them apart from strawberries.

What's the grumbliest bird?
A grouse.

An egg-sit.

Why do storks stand on one leg?
Because if they lifted two they'd fall over.

What's yellow and dangerous?
A canary with a hand grenade.

Which bird can lift the heaviest weight?
A crane.

Which seabird was a famous astronomer?
Gullileo.

Gull-axy

My tern.

What do you get if you cross…

A homing pigeon with a parrot?
A bird that can ask its way if it gets lost.

A cockerel with a poodle in a Chinese restaurant?
Cock-a-noodle-poodle-doodle-oo.

A cow with a duck?
Cream quackers.

A parrot and whale?
A big blubber mouth.

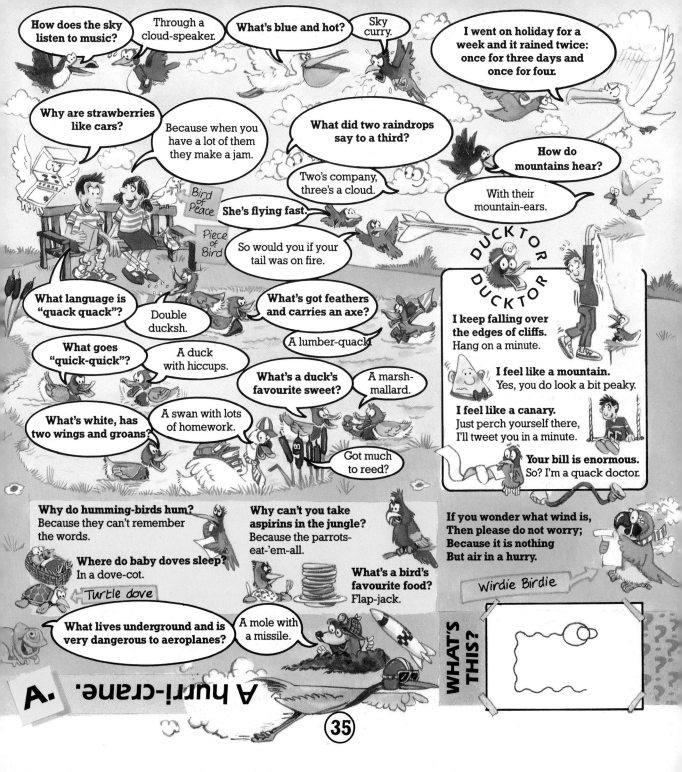

What do you call an anteater who hates ants?
Starving.

Why are camels moody?
Because they've always got the hump.

Heard about the hippy mink?
She was fur out.

What's Australian and calls people names?
A kangar-rude.

What do you call the Australian self-defence expert?
Unarmed Wombat.

What's a polar bear's favourite food?
Iceberg-ers.

What do camels use to wake up in the morning?
A llama clock.

Who's the best known animal in Canada?
Fam-moose.

What's stripey and comes in packs?
Wolves in pyjamas.

Why is a crocodile like a photographer?
They both snap.

What do you get if you cross...

A snake and a spider?
A cobra-web.

An eskimo with a lizard?
An igloo-ana.

A snake with a clown?
Hiss-terical.

An alligator with a chocolate bar?
Chocodile.

A kangeroo and a bear?
A fur coat with pockets.

A cow and a camel?
Lumpy milkshakes.

An aligator with an apple?
Something that bites you first.

A parrot and a hyena?
An animal that laughs at its own jokes.

A crocodile and a rose?
I don't know, but don't try and smell it.

A skunk with a hedgehog?
A porcupong.

A beaver and an eskimo's house?
Something to ig-gnaw.

Why did the snake have a calculator?
It was an adder.

> I do long division.

What do you call an indecisive snake?
A slithery ditherer.

What's a snake's favourite game?
Hiss-chase.

What snake is always fighting?
A battlesnake.

What's a snake's favourite food?
Slither and bacon.

> I thought it was cherry pie-thon.

What do they sing in the desert at Christmas?
O camel ye faithful.

How do you stop a skunk from smelling?
Hold its nose.

What's got big teeth and annoys people?
An agitator-gator.

What kind of fur do you get from a skunk?
As fur as possible.

A duck changing its mind.

Moose is Scottish for mouse.

> Mum, I want to keep my pet skunk under the bed.

> But what about the smell?

> It's OK, he'll get used to it.

Did you hear about the silly penguin? He took his scarf back as it was too tight.

> I'm boared.

Track-oon

Snake charmer

Noah the boa

Which mouse was a Roman emperor?
Julius Cheeser.

What's yellow and goes: PPSSSSSHHHH!
A canary with a puncture.

What's brown and takes aspirin?
A gerbil with a headache.

What are cold and squeaky?
Mice-icles.

What has yellow hair and pants?
A golden retriever after a long walk.

Why did the dog howl?
Because it saw the tree bark.

What's the difference between...

A crazy rabbit and forged banknote?
One's a mad bunny, and the other is bad money.

An escaped guinea pig and a cold?
It's easy to catch a cold.

HOT DOG by Ken L. Alight

A 3-legged koala climbing a giraffe.

When is a brown dog not a brown dog?
When it's a greyhound.

Why do dogs chase sticks?
To look fetching.

What's the biggest mouse in the world?
A hippopota-mouse.

Have you heard about the dalmation actor?
He's in the spotlight.

What do you call a greyhound covered in custard?
A yellowhound.

What looks like a gorilla and goes "squeak"?
A mouse going to a fancy dress party.

Where do young cats live?
Great Kitten.

What's a scaredy cat?
Something that's pet-rified.

What did the cat say when told it was making too much noise?
Me, 'ow?

What's green and jumps out of aeroplanes with a gun?
A parrot-trooper.

What always follows a dog?
Its tail.

There was a pet rabbit from Gloucester,
Whose owners thought they had lost her.
From the fridge came a sound
At last she was found!
The trouble was, how to defrost her.

What do you call a cat...

That steals things?
A cat burglar.

That's got eight legs?
Octo-puss.

That has a cold?
Cat-arrh.

That's pretending to be a flag?
Pole-cat.

DUCKTOR DUCKTOR

QUACK IN 5 MINUTES — Ducktor

I feel like a clock.
You're too wound up.

I keep stealing chairs
Don't take a seat.

I think I'm a door knob.
Don't fly off the handle.

Now I think I'm a keyhole.
I'd better look into it.

I think I'm a telephone.
Take these – if they don't help, give me a ring.

What has 12 legs, three tails and can't see?

Three blind mice.

A is for Alsatian
B is for Bird
C is for Cat
D is for Dog

What's this?

An alpha-pet.

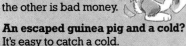

Q. Why don't goats eat jokes?

What do you call a deer who can see well?
A good eye-deer.

What did the horse say when its lunch vanished?
Hay presto!

Why don't cows close doors?
Because they were born in a barn.

 **How many sheep make a sweater?**
None, sheep can't knit.

Why did the cow eat money?
So she could produce rich milk.

 Why did the duckpond shake?
Because there was an earth-quack.

KNOCK! KNOCK! WHO'S THERE?

Ee-aw.
Ee-aw who?
Ee-awta let me in.

What do you get if you cross...

Two deer with an extinct bird?
A doe-doe.

A cow with a snake?
A puff-udder.

A cow with an octopus?
An animal that milks itself.

A bull with a sleeping pill?
A bull-dozer.

What do you call a very clever mare?
An expert in her field.

What food is good for horses and pigs?
Hay-corns.

What do you call a horse that's been all round the world?
A globe-trotter.

Why did the foal cough?
Because it was a little hoarse.

What's got four legs and can see just as well at both ends?
A horse with its eyes closed.

How do you hire a horse?
Make it wear stilts.

Where do sheep go on holiday?
The baa-amas.

Where do lambs like to shop?
Wool-worths.

You can always find a baa-gain.

HORSE TALK by Winnie-Ann Nay

Clothes horse

TRADITIONAL TRANSPORT by ORSON KARTE

What goes 'aab-aab'?
A sheep running backwards?

A stick insect in a fluffy jumper.

Central bleating.

How do sheep keep warm in winter?

My warren's got bugs, Bunny.

What do you get from a sheep who loves karate?
Lamb chops.

40

What fish is always asleep?

What do you call a stupid squid?
A squidiot.

What comes after a sea-horse?
A dee-horse.

What's on the sea-bed and made of chocolate?
An oyster egg.

What's the difference between a ton and the ocean?
Weight and sea.

What were the whale's children called?
Blubber and sister.

What whale is quackers?
Moby Duck.

How do baby fish swim?
They do the crawl.

Who ate his victims two by two?
Noah Shark.

How do squid get to work?
On an octobus.

What happened when the stupid turtle washed its shell?
It broke the washing-machine.

What bus crossed the ocean?
Colum-bus.

Where do fish borrow money?
From a loan shark.

What's yellow, full of holes and holds water?
A sponge.

How do you confuse an octopus?
Tell it to count to nine on its fingers.

How can you tell a stupid fish?
It shelters under a bridge when it's raining.

And it wears a plastic mac-kerel.

What goes dot, dot, dash?
Morse cod.

I want to hold your hand, your hand, your hand...

What did the octopus say to her boyfriend?

Why didn't the prawn put anything in the collection tin?
Because it was a little shellfish.

Piano tuna

What can fall on the sea without getting wet?
Your shadow.

What fish leaves footprints on the sea-bed?
A sole.

Have you heard about the Dead Sea?
I didn't even know it was ill.

Fish cake

A stick.

Why did the sea roar?
Wouldn't you if you had lobsters on your bottom?

Glam clam

What's a hound's favourite dance?
The fox trot.

What has long ears and an engine?
A hare-oplane.

How do hedgehogs play leapfrog?
Very carefully.

What's black and white and goes very fast?
A turbo badger.

What's small, spotted and eats mud?
The lesser spotted mud muncher.

Why did the fox sleep on its back?
To keep its tennis shoes dry.

KNOCK! KNOCK! WHO'S THERE?

A spider.
A spider who?
A spider light on so I know you're in.

Heifer.
Heifer who?
Heifer cow is better than none.

Quacker.
Quacker who?
Quacker nother joke and I'm going.

Weevil.
Weevil who?
Weevil see.

Why was the centipede late for the game of football?
It took her two hours to put on her boots.

What happened when the magician changed a plug?
He changed it into a rabbit.

It was an elec-trick.

What did the squirrel say at the end of its hibernation?
Is it half past March already?

DUCKTOR DUCKTOR

For ten years my brother has thought he was a cow.
Why didn't you bring him to me earlier?
We've saved loads of money on milk.

Will you take my temperature?
Why, I've got one of my own?

What's nice to mice?
A lazy squeak-end.

Which part of a fish weighs the most?
The scales.

Where do beavers keep their money?
In a river bank.

Who's the most famous underwater spy?
James Pond.

Why are fishermen like mad dogs?
They're always wanting a bite.

What goes into the water green and comes out blue?
A frog on a cold day.

What's the best way to catch a fish?
Get someone to throw you one.

What do you call a baby crayfish?
A nipper.

Why did the water smell?
It was a duck ponged.

Duck!

I know I am.

The skeleton of a jellyfish.

MICE NIGHTMARES BY I.C.A. Trapp

COW HORROR FILMS by B. Featers

FROG HOBBIES by Leigh Ping

I've got a person in my throat.

FROG CHAIRS by Lilly Padd

SAFE ROAD CROSSINGS BY Luke Left & Den Wright

Spike one!

Goat of arms | Fox glove

Deer stalker | Deers talking

Where do you find a spider with no legs?
Exactly where you left it.

What can never be made right?
A grasshopper's left eye.

Why do bees hum?
Because they don't know the words

Why did the fly fly?
Because the spider spied 'er.

What's got no teeth and lives in a brick?
A stupid woodworm.

What's green and hairy and shouts 'Help!'?
A caterpillar in a pond.

Why do swallows fly south for the winter?
Because it's too far to walk.

SOUTH

Why did the bird sleep under the car?
To catch the oily worm.

What did the crow say when it laid a square egg?
Ouch!

Which is the sweetest bird on the pond?
A coot.

What did the ram say to his girlfriend?
I love ewe.

What do you call a young sheep that works in a bar?
A baa-lamb.

Why did the one-armed farmer limp into his burning house?
To rescue his lucky horseshoe.

When is a cow like a chef?
When it's calving.

What do cows do after an earthquake?
Produce milk shakes.

Why did the cow play the violin during milking?
She was a moo-sician.

I love Moo-zart.

Why did the farmer run a herd of cows over her field?
She wanted mashed potatoes.

Why don't rabbits buy holes?
Because they can always burrow them.

What do you call a rabbit that works in a barbers?
A hare-dresser.

How do you stop rabbits digging up your garden?
Hide the spade.

Bunion

What does an overweight rabbit do when it rains?
Gets wet.

When is a toad the happiest?
In a leap year.

Where do frogs fly their flags?
On tadpoles.

I like hop scotch.

What's a rabbit's favourite place?
A bun-fair.

I love the mole-er coaster!

Can Caterpillar come out to play?

No, she's just changing.

What are spiders' webs no good for?
Flies.

Why was the spider on television?
She read the webber forecast.

What game do flies hate most?
Squash.

What has fifty legs but can't walk?
Half a centipede.

A. In the croakroom.

WHAT'S THIS?

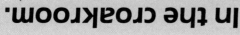

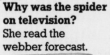

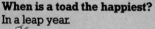

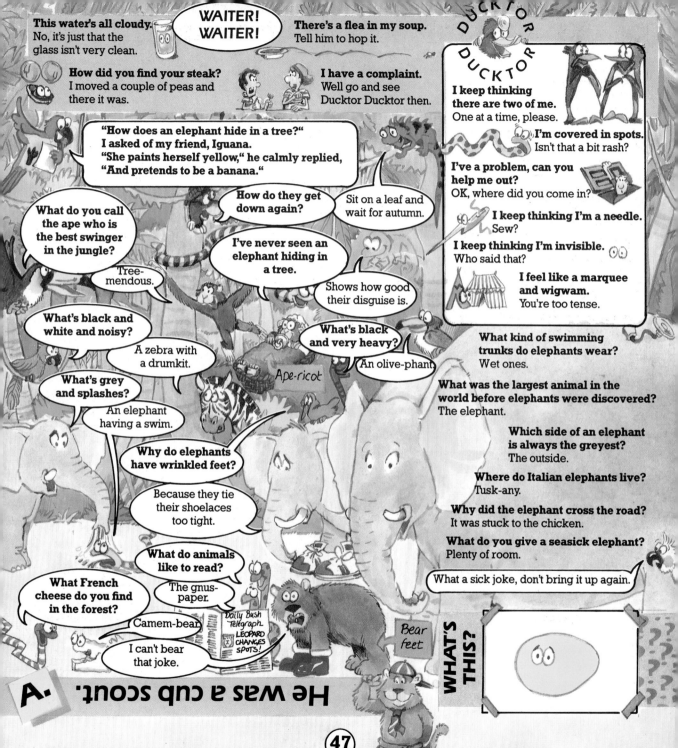

This water's all cloudy.
No, it's just that the glass isn't very clean.

WAITER! WAITER!

There's a flea in my soup.
Tell him to hop it.

How did you find your steak?
I moved a couple of peas and there it was.

I have a complaint.
Well go and see Ducktor Ducktor then.

DUCKTOR DUCKTOR

I keep thinking there are two of me.
One at a time, please.

I'm covered in spots.
Isn't that a bit rash?

I've a problem, can you help me out?
OK, where did you come in?

I keep thinking I'm a needle.
Sew?

I keep thinking I'm invisible.
Who said that?

I feel like a marquee and wigwam.
You're too tense.

"How does an elephant hide in a tree?"
I asked of my friend, Iguana.
"She paints herself yellow," he calmly replied,
"And pretends to be a banana."

What do you call the ape who is the best swinger in the jungle?
Tree-mendous.

How do they get down again?
Sit on a leaf and wait for autumn.

I've never seen an elephant hiding in a tree.
Shows how good their disguise is.

What's black and white and noisy?
A zebra with a drumkit.

What's black and very heavy?
An olive-phant.

What's grey and splashes?
An elephant having a swim.

Ape-ricot

What kind of swimming trunks do elephants wear?
Wet ones.

What was the largest animal in the world before elephants were discovered?
The elephant.

Which side of an elephant is always the greyest?
The outside.

Where do Italian elephants live?
Tusk-any.

Why do elephants have wrinkled feet?
Because they tie their shoelaces too tight.

Why did the elephant cross the road?
It was stuck to the chicken.

What do you give a seasick elephant?
Plenty of room.

What do animals like to read?
The gnus-paper.

What French cheese do you find in the forest?
Camem-bear.

I can't bear that joke.

Daily Bush Telegraph
LEOPARD CHANGES SPOTS!

Bear feet

What a sick joke, don't bring it up again.

A. He was a cub scout.

WHAT'S THIS?

Why did the flea live on the dog's chin?
Because he liked a woof over his head.

What's big and hairy, and over 2,000 miles long?
The Ape Wall of China.

What jumps and collects pollen?
A walla-bee.

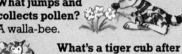

What's a tiger cub after it's fourteen days old?
Fifteen days old.

Why can't famous leopards lead a quiet life?
Because they are always spotted.

What's pink and slimy and weighs 4 tons?
An inside out elephant.

Where do woodpeckers leave their cars?
In the car bark.

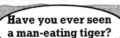

Have you ever seen a man-eating tiger?

No, but I've seen a woman eating yoghurt.

What are you doing?

Just lion around.

A sleepy pigeon looking down a hole.

What do you get if you cross…

A jellyfish with a T.V.?
A jellyfish-on.

A shellfish with a rooster?
Cockle-doodle-do.

A shark with the Loch Ness monster?
Loch jaws.

A whale and a cabbage?
Brussel spouts.

WHALE HORROR STORIES by R. Poon

I wish I could spit out of the top of my head.

A fish with a gangster?
The Codfather.

I thought it was a lobster mobster.

A red mullet with a blue shark?
I don't know, but it's purple.

The ocean with a paper boat?
Wet.

A shrimp with a limpet?
A cling prawn.

An icicle with a fierce dog?
Frost bite.

A shellfish with a sheep?
A clam chop.

An oyster with a cat?
A purrl.

A squid with eight cats?
An octo-pus.

FISH SQUASH by Sir Dean Tinn

Why do donkeys go to bed?
Because the bed won't come to them.

What sound do hedgehogs make when they kiss?
Ouch! Ow! Agh!

When are mountain goats most successful?
When they reach their peak.

What's small and squeaks and has a key?
A door-mouse.

What's worse than a giraffe with a sore throat?
A centipede with in-growing toe-nails.

Can you fly faster than a train?
Of course, trains can't fly.

Why couldn't the boy fit an elephant into a match box?
He forgot to take the matches out first.

Do you like bison?

I don't know, I've never bised.

Name nine animals from Africa.

Eight elephants and a giraffe.

Hari fishna

Angel fish

Goodby

Halo.

Keep your big mouth shut and we won't get caught.

What's big and ugly and goes "beeep!"?
A monster in a traffic jam.

Why couldn't the caveman sleep?
Because of the dino-snores.

How do you make a shepherd's pie for a monster?
Take three shepherds . . .

What have a car and a mammoth got in common?
They've both got wheels except the mammoth.

What do apes have with their coffee?
A sneezy.

What's the biggest ghost in the world?
An ele-phantom.

I'm reading my horror-scope.

What has six legs, four ears and stripes?
A girl on a zebra.

What has two heads, three horns and five legs?
A buffalo with spare parts.

What's stripy and has 16 wheels?
A zebra on roller skates.

What's black and white and eats like a horse?
A zebra.

Giraffe has a long neck,
So it's said,
To join its body
To its head.

Bee-ver

A. The low-end.

What's the difference between...

A buffalo and a bison?
You can't wash in a buffalo.

An elephant and spaghetti?
An elephant doesn't slip off the fork.

A biscuit and an elephant?
You can't dip an elephant in your tea.

An elephant and a pillow?
A pillow never remembers.

An Indian elephant and an African elephant?
About 10,000 kilometres.

WAITER! WAITER!

Do you have chicken legs?
No, I always walk like this.

Do you have wild duck?
No, but I could find a calm one and annoy it for you.

What's this in my soup?
I don't know – all insects look the same to me.

Do they ever change the tablecloths in this restaurant?
I don't know, I've only been here a year.

My plate's wet.
That's the soup.

Will my pizza be long?
No, round.

Restaurant
PERSON NEEDED TO LAY TABLES

What do you call an elephant in the sky?
A thunder cloud.

What monkey is like a flower?
A chimp-pansy.

Where do ant-eaters like to eat?
In a restaur-ant.
MENU

What do you call a deer with no eyes?
No i-dea.

What do you call a deer with no eyes or legs?
Still no i-dea.

What did the tiger say to his girlfriend?
I'm wild about you.

I've a purple nose, three eyes and five green ears – what am I?
Very ugly.

Dad! There's a kangeroo at the door.
Tell him to hop it.

I've just had a bad dream about a horse.
It must have been a night-mare.

What do you get if you cross a brontosaurus with a very old carton of milk?
A dino-sour.

What gets bigger the more you take from it?
My hole.

WHAT'S THIS?

(53)

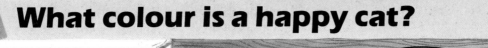

What's got four legs, a shell and fangs?
A terror-pin.

Why was the guinea pig carrying an umbrella?
Because it had forgotten its raincoat.

How did the budgie get to work?
In a budgeri-car.

What's the definition of a toilet?
A jacuzzi for hamsters.

What's brown, flies and wears red underwear?
Super-Gerbil.

What's gold and has a snorkel?
A confused goldfish.

What do you get if you cross...

An alsatian with an oven?
A hot dog.

A labrador with a telephone?
A golden receiver.

A pet dog with a bear?
Winnie-the-Poodle.

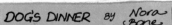
DOG'S DINNER BY Nora Bone

THE NAUGHTY KITTEN by Claude Sofa

A whaleway.

Mary had a little cat,
Peter had a pup,
Chrissy had a crocodile
Which ate the others up.

What's yellow and croaks?
A canary with a cold.

What's yellow and smells?
A canary eating garlic

Why did the cat put her kittens in the drawer?
Because you shouldn't leave litter lying around.

What does a Grand Prix cat sound like?
mmeeEEOOooowww!
It runs on pet-rol.

What pets make the most noise?
Trum-pets.

What's grey, buzzes and eats cheese?
A mouse-quito.

What's brown on the top, white on the bottom and goes: "Eeek!"
A mouse sitting on an ice-cube.

What's white and goes round and round?
A mouse in a washing machine.
I was grey when I went in.

What's the main ingredient in dog biscuits?
Collie-flour.

What's the definition of a cat-flap?
A cat trying to be a bat.

woof-les

watch dog

How did you get on in the milk-drinking contest?
I won by six laps.

What do you call...

A rabbit with its ear in a plug socket?
A current bunny.

A cat that's not house-trained?
Tiddles.

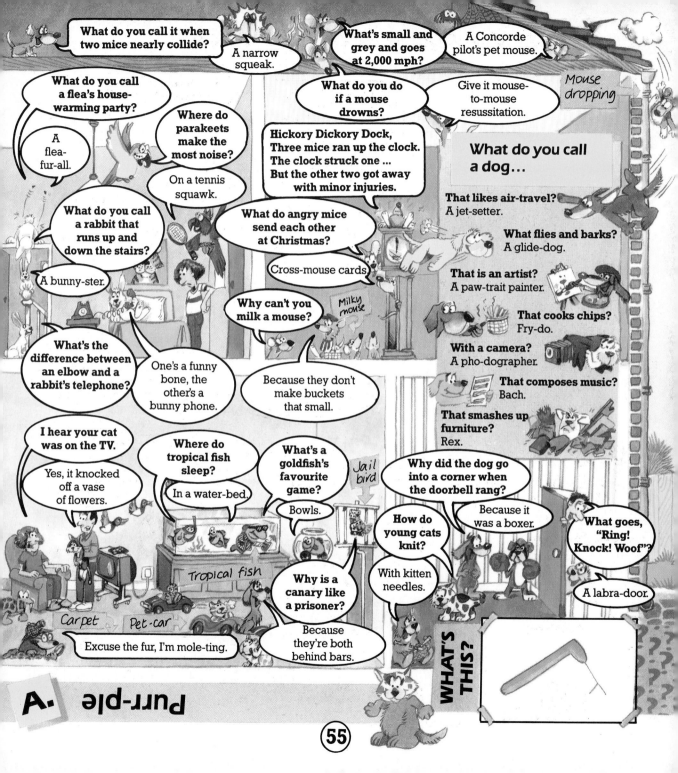

Menu

What's small, has six legs and breathes fire.
A dragon-fly.

What goes 'bzzzniff'?
A hornet with hay fever.

What do you call a line of five mosquitoes?
A mosqui-foot.

Which fly do you find on a building site?
A crane-fly.

What has lots of legs and wears perfume?
A scentipede.

What's the most timid insect?
Mayfly.

Bee-ginner

ABC

Gee.

What about D,E and F?

BEE-WARE

Bee-stly

Bee-autiful

Bee-fy

Why do bees have sticky hair?
Because they have honey combs.

How do bees get to work?
By buzz.

'Bye buzz!

What do bees say when they get in from work?
Honey, I'm home.

What's worse than being with a fool?
Fooling with a bee.

Where do you put a crazy snail?
In a nut-shell.

What do you get if you take away a stick insect's tea?
A sick insect.

I always eat peas with honey,
I've done it all my life.
It makes the peas taste funny,
But it keeps them on the knife.

What did the woodworm say when she saw Pinocchio?
Dinner time!

What's got six legs, a long tongue and makes pizzas?
A butterfly (I lied about the pizzas).

What's yellow and black and speaks very quietly?
A wasper.

BEE KEEPING by Ivan Ive

What's a worm's favourite food?
Mud pie.

What marches round a fort on 100 legs?
A sentry-pede.

What is a beetle's favourite pop group?
The Humans.

Why didn't the woodworm eat the sofa and armchair?
Because he didn't like to eat suites between meals.

How do beetles tell the time?
With a clock-roach.

What do you call a scorpion when it gets off a rock?
A scorpioff.

A sheep pretending to be a tree.

INSECTS WITH MANY LEGS by Millie Pede

FROM Caterpillar TO BUTTERFLY by Chris Aliss

BUG HEADGEAR by Anne Tenner

INSECTS
OUTSECTS

Ear-wig go!

Jitterbug

Buggy

Litter bug

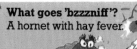

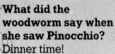

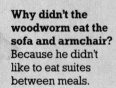

What do you get if you cross...

A bee with a bell?
A hum-dinger.

An elephant and a fly?
An overweight spider.

A spider with a washing line?
A spin-dryer.

A bee with a beetle?
A humbug.

A grasshopper and a hippo?
Craters in your lawn.

An insect with a bird?
A bug-gerigar.

A stick insect with a witch?
A broomstick insect.

A wasp with a big bird?
A buzzard.

A woodworm with a church pew?
Holy furniture.

A snail with an elf?
A shelf.

One, two, flea . . .

I'm good at moth-ematics.

Time flies

Why are you eating a worm?
You told me to do a bird impression.

A. ˙oɹʇs-ǝǝq ɐ ʇ∀

BUG BOTTLE

What did the caterpillar say when he saw a butterfly?
You'll never get me up in one of those things.

What do you call a fly when it retires?
A flew.

What has antlers, flies and bites?
A moose-quito.

What's got six legs and always does its homework?
A fly swat.

What insect drinks the most?
A beer-wig.

What's looks like a grasshopper and wears a blue hat?
A grasshopper in a blue hat.

What do snails use to make their shells shiny?
Snail polish.

Moss-quito

Waiter! Waiter! There's no fly in my soup.

Heard about the two tarantulas that got married?
It was a lovely webbing.

What's got eight legs, two wheels and goes very fast?
A spider on a motorbike.

What do you call a spider with no legs?
A currant.

What do you get if you cross a tennis court with a snail?
A lot older.

Which insect is always the best at school?
A tick.

10 - 7 = 3 ✓

Why was the ground wet?
Because the centipede.

What's the difference between a worm and an apple?
I don't know, what?
I'm never going to ask you to make an apple pie.

WHAT'S THIS?

59

What lion never roars?

What do you call a hippopotamus with chicken pox?
A hippo-spotty-mus.

What's green and wobbles?
A lizard on a tightrope.

What motorbike does a hyena ride?
A Yama-ha-ha.

How do you hunt bear?
Take your clothes off.

Why don't hippos eat clocks?
It's too time-consuming.

What do you call a puma from Poland?
A pole-cat.

Algy met a bear,
The bear met Algy.
The bear was bulgy,
The bulge was Algy.

Bat-minton

How do you open a monk's door?
With a monk-key.

What are the most expensive animals?
Deer.

How did the animals escape from the shipwreck?
On a gir-raft.

Tie-ger

An ant with bad breath.

What do you get if you cross...

A dinner service with an alligator?
A crockery-dile.

A cheetah with a jet?
I don't know, no-one's ever caught one.

A giraffe and a watchdog?
Something that barks at low-flying aircraft.

A hippopotamus with a potato?
A chippo.

A stupid gorilla and a kangaroo?
A big, thick jumper.

A leopard with firewood?
A cat-a-log.

A fish and two elephants?
Swimming trunks.

A giraffe with a hedgehog?
A long-handled toothbrush.

An elephant with a cup of coffee?
A drink that never forgets.

A bear and a skunk?
Winnie-the-Pooh.

An elephant with a crow?
Broken telegraph poles.

A watchdog and a tiger?
A nervous postman.

An elephant and a light bulb?
A large electricity bill.

An elephant with an encyclopedia?
A big know-all.

A large elk and a fruit?
Strawberry moose.

How do you make an elephant split?
Ice cream, cherries, chocolate sauce, elephant ...

How do you make an elephant sandwich?
First, take a big loaf of bread...

What's the best place buy an elephant?
Jumbo sale.

What do you call a toothless elephant?
Gumbo.

KNOCK! KNOCK! WHO'S THERE?

Lionel.
Lionel who?
Lionel bite you if you don't watch out.

What did the skunk say when the wind changed directions?
Phaw!

What's green and flies?
The jungle in a helicopter.

What do gazelles have that no other animal has?
Baby gazelles.

HOW NOT TO MEET LIONS — BY — Claudia Leggov

CLUMSY ELEPHANT by Stan Don McComs

BOUNDING THROUGH THE JUNGLE BY Anne T. Lope

POISONOUS SNAKES by Leigh Thall

What do you call a big monkey who likes sweets?
A meringue-utang.

What's yellow, then green, then yellow?
A banana working part-time as a cucumber.

What's yellow and points north?
A magnetic banana.

What goes thud, squelch, thud, squelch?
A peanut with one wet shoe.

What's blue and square?
A banana in disguise.

What's the hardest food to eat?
A banana – sideways.

Why are bananas yellow?
So they can hide in custard.

What do monkeys sing at Christmas?
Jungle bells.

What would you rather ate you, a lion or a gorilla?
I'd rather the lion ate the gorilla.

What do you do if a gorilla tells you a joke?
Laugh very loudly.

What deer can you see through?
A win-doe.

Heard about the fireflies who met at sunrise?
It was love at first light.

How do you begin a letter to a stag?
Deer Stag, ...

What plays the trumpet and hisses?
A brass-snake.

Who was the famous monkey general?
Ape-oleon Baboon-aparte.

Why do tigers eat raw meat?
Because they don't know how to cook.

What's the best way to talk to an angry tiger?
Long distance.

What's bright blue and very, very heavy?
An elephant holding its breath.

What's a moose's favourite fruit?
Mooseberries.

What do French geese wear?
Goose-berets.

How do you know when there's an elephant ...

At a barbeque?
He's the one with the biggest ribs.

In your garden?
Peanut shells in the shed.

In your family?
You can never get into the bathroom.

In the custard?
When it's very lumpy.

In the oven?
You can't get the door shut.

What's black, white and red?

A panther eating a strawberry sandwich.

A zebra with a nose bleed.

A sunburnt polar bear with dirty paws.

Hi Ena.

'Ello Phant.

Bad spelling rools O.K

Queen Elizabeth II rules U.K.

Goblin food is bad for the elf....

Esc-ape

FOR THE TEN MILLIONTH TIME – DON'T EXAGGERATE!

Ape-ron

What has a long neck and writes on walls? Giraffiti

People with bad memories are....er.....um..

How do you record an ape?
On an ape recorder.

Rock 'n' mole

A dandelion.

61

On these two pages are lots of ideas for how you can make up your own jokes about animals, birds, insects, fish and reptiles.

Jokes using animal puns

A pun is when all or part of a word is replaced with a word that sounds like it. For example in this joke:
What do cats like for their birthday?
Purr-fume.
(The first part of the word perfume has been replaced.)

> A pun is sometimes called a play on words.

Think of an animal (the shorter the better). → Sheep

Write down all the other words you can think of that are connected to it. → Baa, lamb, wool, fleece, chop, bleat

For each one, write down words, or parts of words, that sound similar to it. → Baa: *Bar*, *bar*becue, *bar*bara, *bar*bells, *bar*maid, *bar*n.

Now replace the new word parts with the animal word. → Baa, baa-becue, baa-bara, baa-bells, baa-maid, baa-n.

Think of questions that use the animal and the new pun words. → **What do strong sheep use?** Baa-bells.

> Can you think up jokes for the other pun words?

Here are some other pun words for you to try.

Hen-chanted   Bull-garia   Bee-tle
Hen-ergy   Ass-ma   Chimp-ney

Odd animal descriptions

Quite a few jokes in this book use the idea of an animal doing something odd. For example:
What's got eight legs and puffs?
A spider running a marathon.

Write down an animal, and one description of it. → Leopard – has spots
Beetle – is black
Dog – goes 'woof'

Write down an everyday object. → Calculator
Stilts
Roller skates

Write down what this object would make you do, look like or have. → Be good at sums
Be very tall
Have eight wheels

Write your joke using the animal and object descriptions. → **What is black and very tall?** A beetle on stilts.

> Can you complete the last two? You could also swap the animals and objects around.

Here are some more ideas for odd animal jokes. All you have to do is think of the animal and its description.

What's (description) and goes round and round?
A (animal) in a washing machine.

What's . . . and laughs?
A . . . reading a joke book.

What's . . . and glows?
A 100 watt . . .

What's . . . and has stripes?
Sergeant . . .

Types of joke

On this page you can find out some of the different types of animal joke you can make up.

What do you get if you cross . . .

What do you get if you cross a joke book with geese?
A giggle gaggle.

This type of joke is great fun because you can imagine what you get when you cross animals with other things.

A good way of making up these jokes is to do a joke square. There is one below which has been part-filled in. Try and think of things for each blank square.

Don't worry if some of them don't seem to work very well.

Cross these with these ▼ ▶	Leopard	Gorilla	Hippo	Bee
Pot of glue			Stick in the mud	
Computer		A big, hairy know-all		
Jellyfish	Spot the jellyfish			
A rose				A bee-auty

You could try it with different animals and objects.

Obvious jokes

In these jokes, the answer is the most obvious one, which catches the other person out. The most famous example of this joke is:
Why did the chicken cross the road?
To get to the other side.

Below are some jokes for you to complete:

Why did the (animal) wear black shoes?
Because its blue ones were at the menders.

Why do – wear furry boots?
To keep their feet warm.

What's the difference between . . .

What's the difference between a rhino telling jokes and a lettuce?
One's a funny beast, the other's a bunny feast.

There are many types of this joke. The one above uses two words that make sense when the first letters are swapped round. (This is called a spoonerism.)

Cat flap – flat cap   **Hiss mystery – miss history**

A note on making up jokes

Jokes can come in two ways: easily and with great difficulty. Sometimes a joke seems to drop into your head from nowhere. But most of the time you will need to work hard to make them up.

The thing to remember is: don't give up!

Knock! Waiter! Doctor!

These three types of joke can also include animals. Here are some ideas for each type which you can use to make up more jokes:

Knock! Knock!

Noah (Know a . . .)
Atch (Atch-oo . . .)
Ernie (Any . . .)
William (Will you . . .)
Howard (How would . . .)
Shirley (Surely . . .)
Sarah ('S there a . . .)
Alison (I listen . . .)
Noel (Know all . . .)

Waiter! Waiter!

There's a dead fly in my soup.
What's this fly doing in my soup?
Your sleeve's in my soup.
Do you have frog's legs?

Doctor! Doctor!

I feel run down.
People keep disagreeing with me.
My nose keeps running.
I keep losing my memory.

A. A comedi-hen

What does it say on the sign outside the haunted hive?
Bee-ware.

Heard about the dog skeleton?
It was always burying itself.

Why don't dragons like knights?
Because they can't stand tinned food.

What animal was the noisiest sleeper?
A bronto-snoreus.

What does a cow ghost say?
Mooooooooooo!

What do you call a mad sheep?
Baa-my.

KNOCK! KNOCK! WHO'S THERE?

Weirdo.
Weirdo who?
Weirdo you think you've been?

Thumping.
Thumping who?
Thumping with big teeth is climbing up your neck.

Howie.
Howie who?
I'm all right, how are you?

What do you get if you cross...

An angry monster with a pet bird?
A budgeri-grrrrr!

A lion with a graveyard?
The cata-tombs.

A dragon with an insect?
A fire-fly.

Why couldn't the dog act with a ghost?
Because he got stage fright.

Alas, poor ostrich . . .

Are you famous?

I'm a nobody.

Nice cos-tomb.

What did the monster call his pet hippo?
Dinner.

What's grey and covered in feathers?
An elephant standing next to an exploding chicken.

What's white and as tall as a giraffe?
A giraffe ghost.

What swims and makes a ghostly noise?
A whale.

What do you call an Australian ghost?
A kangar-ghoul.

They live in the Northern Terror-tory.

What do wolf ghosts think of dracula films?
Fangtastic.

What's black and white and lives in Scotland?
The Loch Ness Zebra.

What's brown and hairy and goes 'slam, slam, slam, slam'?
A four-door gorilla.

Famous animal last words

A monkey:
Who put grease on the treeeeeeeee!

A fish:
Who pulled out the plug?

A squirrel that thought it was a bird:
It's easy, you just flap your arms and....

A worm:
You're up early..

A woodpecker:
Of course this isn't an exploding tree.

A hedgehog:
What's that rumbling noise?

What time is it when you meet a hungry monster?
Time to run.

Let's fly, flea.

Let's flee, fly.

What tunnels through earth and smells rotten?

Mole-dy.